KILLERS OF THE ANIMAL KINGDOM

ORCAS

ELIZABETH KRAJNIK

PowerKiDS
press

New York

Published in 2020 by The Rosen Publishing Group, Inc.
29 East 21st Street, New York, NY 10010

First Edition

Editor: Elizabeth Krajnik
Book Design: Reann Nye

Photo Credits: Cover Grafissimo/E+/Getty Images; pp. 4, 5, 15, 21 Tory Kallman/Shutterstock.com; p. 6 wildestanimal/Shutterstock.com; p. 7 Greg Schneider/birdphotographer.ca/Moment/Getty Images; p. 9 Foto 4440/Shutterstock.com; p. 10 MR1805/iStock / Getty Images Plus/Getty Images; pp. 11, 12 Monika Wieland Shields/Shutterstock.com; p. 13 Agami Photo Agency/Shutterstock.com; p. 14 Mike Korostelev www.mkorostelev.com/Moment/Getty Images; p. 17 Neirfy/Shutterstock.com; p. 18 nodff/Shutterstock.com; p. 19 Ingus Kruklitis/Shutterstock.com; p. 20 Lazareva/iStock / Getty Images Plus/Getty Images; p. 22 Christian Musat/Shutterstock.com.

Cataloging-in-Publication Data

Names: Krajnik, Elizabeth.
Title: Orcas / Elizabeth Krajnik.
Description: New York : PowerKids Press, 2020. | Series: Killers of the animal kingdom| Includes glossary and index.
Identifiers: ISBN 9781725306172 (pbk.) | ISBN 9781725306196 (library bound) | ISBN 9781725306189 (6pack)
Subjects: LCSH: Killer whale–Juvenile literature.
Classification: LCC QL737.C432 K73 2020 | DDC 599.53'6–dc23

Manufactured in the United States of America

CPSIA Compliance Information: Batch #CSPK19. For Further Information contact Rosen Publishing, New York, New York at 1-800-237-9932.

CONTENTS

Killer Whales 4

Orca Basics. 6

On the Hunt 8

Pod Communication 10

Killer Calves 12

Orca Ecotypes 14

Orcas and Humans. 16

Captive Orcas 18

Conservation Efforts 20

Saving Killer Whales 22

Glossary 23

Index 24

Websites. 24

KILLER WHALES

Orcas, which are commonly called killer whales, aren't actually whales. They're the largest members of the dolphin family. However, these giant **mammals** are one of the most powerful predators on Earth. Orcas are very smart and have a number of **adaptations** that make them such good killers.

Over the years, orcas have gotten a bad **reputation** for killing people. However, orca attacks have only happened in cases of orcas held in **captivity**. Wild animals aren't meant to live in captivity and, as a result, orcas are sometimes misunderstood and feared. Read on to learn the truth about these skilled predators.

Orcas may breach, or leap out of the water, for a number of reasons, including to **communicate** with other orcas and also as a form of play.

5

ORCA BASICS

Orcas have black bodies with white bellies, white parts near their eyes, and a gray part behind their dorsal fin. Male orcas weigh up to 11.02 tons (10 mt) and can be as long as 30 feet (9.1 m). Their dorsal fin can be as tall as 6.5 feet (2 m) high.

KILLER FACTS

In the wild, male orcas live an average of 30 years and females live an average of 46 years. Captive orcas in the United States only live an average of 12 years.

The San Juan Islands in Washington State are a great place to see orcas in the wild from late May to mid-October.

Female orcas weigh up to 8.3 tons (7.5 mt) and can be as long as 27.8 feet (8.5 m). Their dorsal fin is about half the height of male dorsal fins. Orca babies, which are called calves, can weigh up to 400 pounds (181 kg) and are about 7.8 feet (2.4 m) long at birth.

7

ON THE HUNT

Orcas are apex predators, which means they have no natural predators and are at the top of the food chain. They eat fish, penguins, seals, sea lions, whales, squid, and sea birds. Orcas hunt as a pod, or family group. Pods vary in size but may have as many as 40 members.

Pods use different hunting methods to catch their **prey**. To catch seals on pieces of ice, orcas swim together to make a wave. Then, they swim under the piece of ice and push the wave with their tails. The water pushes the seal off the ice, allowing the orcas to attack.

KILLER FACTS

When orcas hunt large prey, such as whales, they often go after young or weak animals. They swim into, bite, and pull on their prey to wear it down.

8

Some orcas living off the coast of Patagonia's Valdes Peninsula purposely go up on the pebbled beach to catch sea lions. They are the only group of orcas known to do this.

POD COMMUNICATION

To hunt, orca pods have to communicate well. Orcas make a number of sounds to communicate with their pods. Some of these sounds are **unique** to members of their pod and can be understood from far away. Different pods may share some of the same sounds. However, no two pods use exactly the same sounds all the time.

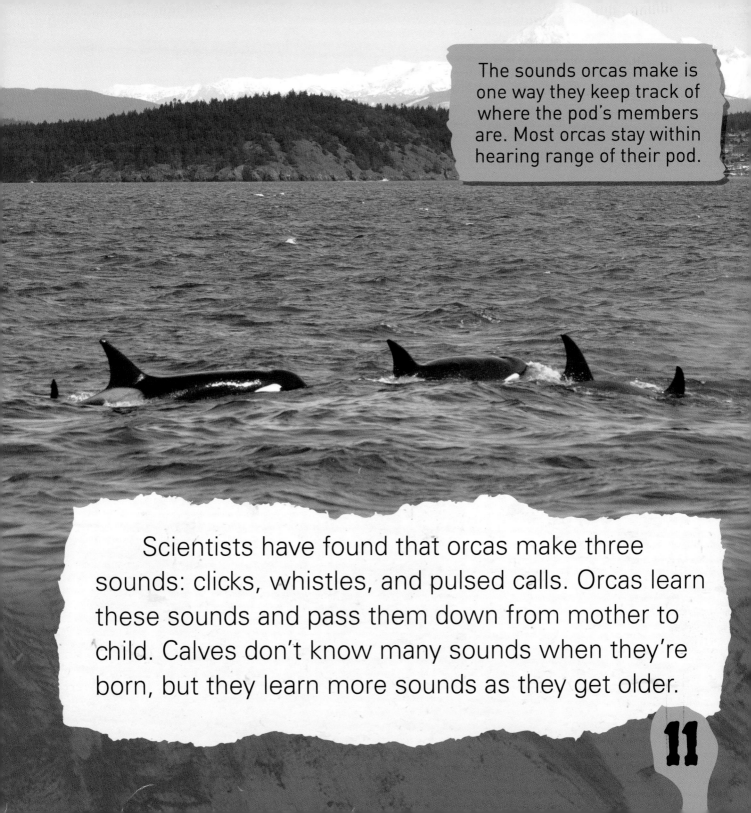

The sounds orcas make is one way they keep track of where the pod's members are. Most orcas stay within hearing range of their pod.

Scientists have found that orcas make three sounds: clicks, whistles, and pulsed calls. Orcas learn these sounds and pass them down from mother to child. Calves don't know many sounds when they're born, but they learn more sounds as they get older.

KILLER CALVES

Orcas usually have babies once every three to five years. However, some orcas may only have a calf once every 10 years. Orcas carry their babies for 17 months on average. They usually give birth to one calf at a time. Calves are born in the water and usually come out of their mother tail first. However, some calves have been born head first.

Calves swim next to their mother to save energy. If they didn't, they might not be able to keep up with the rest of the pod.

At birth, orca calves have a soft dorsal fin and tail **flukes**, which stiffen over time. The white parts of orca calves may look more like pale yellow or tan until the end of the first year. Calves drink their mothers' milk for about a year.

13

ORCA ECOTYPES

Scientists have found different types of orcas, called ecotypes. Orcas belonging to different ecotypes are different sizes, look different, eat different prey, have different communicative sounds, and act differently. Scientists can tell these ecotypes apart by where they live.

KILLER FACTS

Orcas that eat only fish are called fish specialists. Resident orcas eat different types of fish depending on where they live. Generalist orcas eat both fish and mammals.

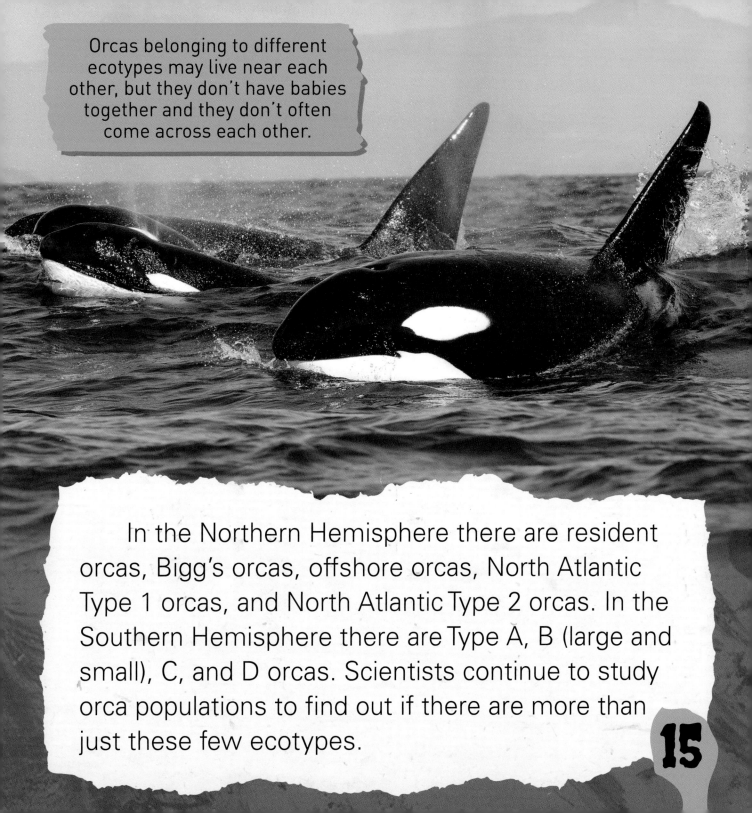

Orcas belonging to different ecotypes may live near each other, but they don't have babies together and they don't often come across each other.

In the Northern Hemisphere there are resident orcas, Bigg's orcas, offshore orcas, North Atlantic Type 1 orcas, and North Atlantic Type 2 orcas. In the Southern Hemisphere there are Type A, B (large and small), C, and D orcas. Scientists continue to study orca populations to find out if there are more than just these few ecotypes.

15

ORCAS AND HUMANS

Humans and orcas have an interesting past. Some humans thought of them as pests. Other humans hunted orcas to make oil from their **blubber**, but orcas don't produce much oil. People and orcas seem to have worked together in the past. Orcas would let humans know large whales were near. Other orcas would help people carry the bodies of large whales.

In the more recent past, humans have almost become **obsessed** with orcas. We see how they act and feel connected to them in some ways. They have strong family ties and so do humans. However, our interest hasn't been good for orcas.

KILLER FACTS

Ted Griffin was famous for capturing orcas. In March 1966, he wrote an article for *National Geographic* titled "Making Friends with a Killer Whale," which likely added to people's obsession with orcas.

People's obsession with orcas has led to books and movies about them. Some of these movies have shown that captive orcas are treated poorly.

17

CAPTIVE ORCAS

Ted Griffin and Don Goldsberry were among the first people to capture orcas. In October 1965, they trapped 15 orcas off the coast of Washington State. One of these orcas, a female, was named Shamu and was sold to SeaWorld in San Diego, California. More orcas were captured and sold to other marine parks around the world. At these **marine** parks, orcas were trained to do tricks.

KILLER FACTS

Some captive orcas have attacked and even killed their trainers. Tilikum, the orca the documentary *Blackfish* is about, killed two trainers at SeaWorld Orlando.

Even though some captive orcas have killed humans, there have been no reports of orcas killing humans in the wild.

Orcas aren't meant to live in captivity. They need to swim and dive deep. In captivity, orcas become bored and upset and may even hurt themselves. In the wild, orcas have strong family ties. When they're captured, these ties are broken and they get upset.

CONSERVATION EFFORTS

Human activities are hurting orca populations. Some populations, such as the Southern Resident population, don't have enough food to eat, get sick from pollutants in the water and in their food sources, and hear extra noise in the places they live.

Some groups work to conserve, or protect, orca populations. They do this by raising money for **research** groups who work to take care of the issues orcas face. These groups also educate people about those issues. Without conservation efforts, orca populations that are endangered, or close to dying out, may die out completely.

In some areas where orcas live and hunt, such as the inland waters of Washington State, boaters are supposed to follow rules so they don't accidentally hurt orcas.

21

SAVING KILLER WHALES

Being mindful of Earth's many plant and animal lifeforms is important. Pollution affects orcas more than most other ocean life. The choices you make every day have an effect on these amazing creatures. If you're at the grocery store and your dad wants salmon for dinner, you should make sure it isn't king salmon. This is one of the Southern Resident orca's favorite foods.

You can also speak up about what cleaning supplies you use around your home. Ask your parents to start using natural cleaning products so fewer pollutants end up in the water supply. You can also speak out about changes to important laws that protect orcas. The lives of killer whales are in our hands.

GLOSSARY

adaptation: A change in a living thing that helps it live better in its habitat.

blubber: The fat on whales and other large marine mammals.

captivity: For an animal, the state of living somewhere controlled by humans—such as a zoo or aquarium—instead of in the wild.

communicate: To share ideas and feelings through sounds and motions.

fluke: One of two lobes, or rounded parts, of a whale's tail.

mammal: Any warm-blooded animal whose babies drink milk and whose body is covered with hair or fur.

marine: Of or relating to the sea.

obsessed: Thinking or talking about someone or something too much.

prey: An animal hunted by other animals for food.

reputation: The views that are held about something or someone.

research: Careful study that is done to find and report new knowledge about something.

unique: Special or different from anything else.

INDEX

A
appearance, 6, 7, 13

B
babies, 7, 11, 12, 13
breaching, 5

C
captivity, 16, 17, 18, 19
communication, 5, 10, 11

D
diet, 8, 13, 14

H
hunting, 8, 9, 10

P
play, 5

S
SeaWorld, 18
Shamu, 18

T
Tilikum, 18

WEBSITES

Due to the changing nature of Internet links, PowerKids Press has developed an online list of websites related to the subject of this book. This site is updated regularly. Please use this link to access the list: www.powerkidslinks.com/kotak/orcas